My Secret Bully

For Allison, Bennett and Brad and to children everywhere.
Special thanks to Kathy Masarie, Sue Wellman, Theresa Markowitz,
Steve Scholl, Jan Koutsky, Belinda Jaffe, Janet Sittig, Jean Butcher and
my amazing family for their wonderful support of my work.
– T.J.L. –

To Mom for getting me started
and to Ilene for keeping me going.
– A.M. –

Copyright text © 2004 by Trudy Ludwig
Copyright illustrations © 2004 by Abigail Marble

Inquiries should be addressed to:
RiverWood Books, PO Box 3400, Ashland, Oregon 97520.

Printed in Indonesia

First edition: 2004

06 05 04 03   9 8 7 6 5 4 3 2 1

Library of Congress Cataloging-in-Publication Data

Ludwig, Trudy.
My secret bully / story by Trudy Ludwig ; illustrations by Abigail
Marble.-- 1st ed.
p. cm.
Includes bibliographical references (p.)
Summary: A girl confides to her mother that her best friend is treating
her badly, and together they figure out what to do about it. Includes a
note to parents and teachers, as well as related resources.
ISBN 1-883991-89-7 (hardcover)
[1. Bullying--Fiction. 2. Friendship--Fiction.] I. Marble, Abigail,
ill. II. Title.
PZ7.L9763My 2003
[Fic]--dc22
2003016018

MY SECRET
BULLY

Story by Trudy Ludwig

Illustrations
by Abigail Marble

RiverWood Books

FOREWORD

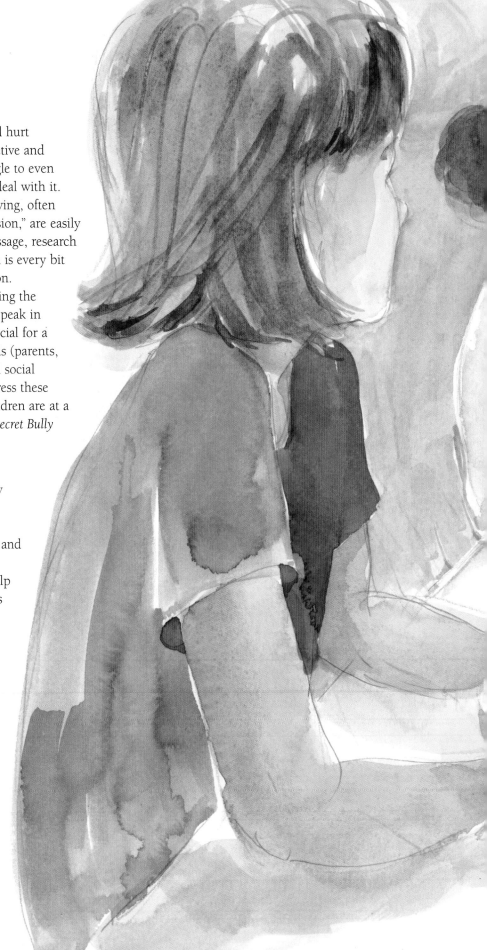

Using relationships to bully and hurt others is by nature covert, secretive and difficult to detect. Adults struggle to even be able to identify it, let alone deal with it. While stories of emotional bullying, often referred to as "relational aggression," are easily dismissed as normal rites of passage, research shows that relational aggression is every bit as harmful as physical aggression. Because bullying is evident during the preschool years and appears to peak in the middle school years, it's crucial for a community of caring individuals (parents, teachers, school counselors and social peers) to come together to address these problems sooner, when the children are at a younger age. That's where *My Secret Bully* comes into play.

My Secret Bully is a touching, inspirational story that instantly draws the young reader into Monica's world, where she is emotionally bullied by a friend and eventually learns how to cope, survive and thrive. With the help of a supportive adult, Monica is given the tools to successfully create her own "happily ever after."

I encourage you to use this story, together with the helpful tips, discussion questions and additional resources listed in the back of the book, as a vehicle for helping others, like Monica, achieve their "happily ever after"—with their self-esteem intact.

Susan Wellman
founder and president of
The Ophelia Project

Katie is my secret bully.

A lot of people would be surprised to know this because they think she's my friend. And she does act like my friend . . . sometimes.

But lately, I'm not so sure.

Katie and I have known each other since kindergarten. We've spent a lot of time together because we like doing the same kinds of things: making perfumes with flowers picked from my yard, playing soccer in the rain, sharing secrets and spying on our bossy, know-it-all brothers.

I love being around Katie when she's nice to me. But there are times when she's not. She can be just plain mean.

And I don't know why.

RECIPES

DAISY PERFUME
12 DAISIES

CLUE

TREASURE

It all started a few months ago, during school recess.
I noticed Katie whispering to a group of girls and
looking at me. I went up to them and asked Katie
what they were talking about.

She said, "Oh nothing,
Mon-ICK-a. I'll tell you later."

Then some of the other girls
giggled like it really was
something, and that made
me feel bad.

The next day, when I was playing with Sarah, Katie grabbed my arm and pulled me away.

"Katie, stop it," I said. "I was talking to Sarah."

"If you play with her," she whispered in my ear, "I won't come over to your house tomorrow."

Then she let go of my arm and skipped away as if nothing happened. But something did happen. And it didn't feel right to me.

I wasn't sure what to do. I really wanted to get together with Katie. But I wanted to play with Sarah, too. So I just ignored what Katie said, thinking maybe she was having a bad day.

A few days later, I saw Katie
playing wallball with Sarah.
It looked like a lot of fun,
so I asked if I could join them.
Katie just stared at me and
didn't say anything. Not one
word.

"Katie?" I asked again. "Can I play
wallball with you and Sarah?"

"We're in the middle of a special
game right now. Maybe later."

I looked at Sarah, hoping she
would change Katie's mind, but
she didn't say anything. Sarah
just stared at her shoes and
pretended I wasn't there. So
I walked away, feeling a tight
knot growing in my belly.

At night, I couldn't concentrate on my homework and my mom noticed. "What's wrong, sweet pea?" she asked.

"I'm having trouble with Katie," I said. "She seems to be really mad at me and I don't know why."

"You've been friends for a long time, Monica. I'm sure you'll work it out," she said.

"I guess . . ." but I really
wasn't so sure.

"Why don't you give her a call and talk to her about it?" mom suggested.

So I did. But when I asked her if she was mad at me for some reason, Katie said, "No, I'm not *mad* at you. You are just *so-o-o-o sensitive* about stuff. Well, I have to do my homework, now. See you later."

Maybe she was right. Maybe I was too sensitive.

Things didn't get any better
after a while. In fact, they got worse.
Much worse. It got to the point where no one
would play with me at recess. I was all by myself.
And there was Katie—hanging out with my other friends,
laughing and being all sweet and nice to everyone . . . but me.

Maybe there
was something
wrong with me.

Last month, for the third day in a row, I told my mom that I had a bad stomachache and didn't feel good enough to go to school.

"You've been complaining of stomachaches a lot lately," she said. "Is something going on at school that's giving you this upset stomach, Monica?"

When I saw the look of love and worry in my mom's eyes, I knew I couldn't keep my secret bully a secret any longer. At first, I just started to cry and couldn't stop. Mom hugged me a lot and waited patiently for me to talk. And I did.

I told her how hard it is to be friends with Katie: "She's nice to me when we're playing alone, but really mean to me when we're around other people. I even think she's been saying bad things about me to my friends so they won't like me," I explained.

I told my mom everything and she listened to what I had to say. I mean—she *really* listened to me. Mom didn't blame me or ask me to be nicer to Katie. And she didn't say, "That's just the way girls are, so you better get used to it," like my babysitter did when I tried to talk to her about it. I felt a lot better after I talked with my mom.

Mom says there are some problems in life that aren't easily solved and this is one of them. But it helps to know that I'm not alone. I found out that a lot of other kids have had this happen to them—even my mom when she was a kid! But that doesn't make it right. And that doesn't mean this is the way it has to be.

Mom and I talked about what I could do to stand up for myself. We even did what mom calls "role-playing," where she acted like she was Katie and I got to practice out loud what I wanted to say to her, without sounding like a bully myself.

So the next day, I was ready. I walked right up to Katie during morning recess, waiting for her to do her worst. She looked at me and started whispering to her circle of friends.

I stared at her straight in the eyes and said, "Katie, does it make you feel good to make me feel bad? Because friends don't do that to friends."

She turned red in the face and looked away. Right then, I knew Katie could no longer hurt me.

I don't see Katie anymore. I feel sad about that,
but now I know that real friends don't treat
each other the way she treated me.
Real friends respect your feelings and
work things out with you when you have
problems. Real friends like you just the
way you are.

Will I ever be friends with Katie again?
I don't think so. I just want to be around
people who really like me.

I'm feeling much better about myself these days.
I've made new friends at school and on my
gymnastics team. And I don't get stomachaches
like I did before. Having a secret bully was
eating up my insides. But now that the
secret's out, I don't feel bad anymore.
It's nice to know that whatever I do,
I'm going to be just fine!

Making A Difference:
A Note To Parents & Teachers

"Relational aggression" refers to acts of emotional bullying hidden among tightly knit networks of friends. Instead of using knives and fists as physical displays of aggression, emotional bullies employ relationships, words and gestures as their preferred weapons of attack.

A bully's reasons for tormenting are as diverse as they are plenty. A child's desire for social connection, recognition and power are key elements used to the aggressor's advantage.

The profiles of the victims run the gamut—from those who are noticeably different in some way from their tormentors (e.g., race, physical appearance and personality) to others who outwardly appear to have much in common with the friends who are bullying them. In some cases, there is no apparent reason why a particular victim is chosen; it may simply be a matter of random selection, based on the bully's sudden need to pick on whomever happens to be in the bully's line of vision.

Common examples of emotional bullying include, but are not limited to, silent treatment, rumors, intimidation, humiliation, exclusion, teasing and manipulation. These types of behaviors can be devastating, resulting in serious injury to the victim's self-esteem and feelings of social unacceptability. Stomachaches, headaches, depression, anxiety and school avoidance are often telltale symptoms of bullied victims.

Unfortunately, many children—both boys and, more prevalently, girls—experience relational aggression at one time or another in their lives. But as Monica in this story comes to find out, "That doesn't make it right. And that doesn't mean this is the way it has to be."

What can we do, as responsible caring adults, to break this vicious cycle of relational aggression? The first step is to bring the secrets of emotional bullying out into the open, so that victims don't feel alone, with no avenue of escape.

The second step is twofold: 1) provide victims with coping tools [refer to the section: What Can A Victim Do?] and 2) prevent further acts of aggression by taking the appropriate measures to quash all forms of overt and covert bullying. Holding bullies accountable for their behavior, as well as recognizing the roles and responsibilities of the victims, bystanders, parents, teachers, administrators, and the community are key to the success of any anti-bullying program.

What Can A Victim Do?

Full Esteem Ahead, an Oregon-based nonprofit organization whose mission is to help create and foster healthy environments for our youth, offers these helpful suggestions:

※ Know that it is not your fault.

※ Know that you don't deserve it.

※ Tell the bully to stop.

※ Remove yourself from the situation.

※ Get help from people you trust.

※ Hang out with people who let you be you.

※ Use humor to deflect bullying.

※ Don't become a bully yourself.

An Opportunity For Discussion

After reading *My Secret Bully*, please use the following questions to generate further discussion with your child or student:

❁ How was Katie being mean to Monica?
  ✽ What did she say?
  ✽ What did she do?

❁ What could Sarah have done to help Monica when Katie was bullying her?

❁ How did Monica stop the bullying?

❁ What else do you think Monica could have done or said?

❁ What would it take for Katie and Monica to become friends again?

❁ Do you think Katie was also being mean to other kids at school?

❁ How are kids mean to each other in your school?

❁ Why are kids mean to each other?

❁ Do boys typically bully others in the same way as girls?

❁ Have you ever been bullied?

❁ How does it feel to be bullied?

❁ What would you do if you saw a friend being bullied by another friend?

Additional Resources

For more information on relational aggression, refer to the following resources:

Organizations

The Empower Program
1312 8th Street, NW
Washington, DC 20001
www.empowered.org

Full Esteem Ahead
10445 SW Canyon Road
Suite 111D
Beaverton, OR 97005
www.fullesteemahead.org

GENaustin
Girl Empowerment Network™
P.O. Box 3122
Austin, TX 78764
www.genaustin.org

The Ophelia Project®
P.O. Box 8736
Erie, PA 16505-0736
www.opheliaproject.org

Bullying Websites

www.bullying.org

www.no-bully.com

www.stopbullyingme.ab.ca/

www.stopbullyingnow.com

www.lfcc.on.ca/bully.htm

Recommended Readings

For Adults:

Coloroso, Barbara. *The Bully, the Bullied, and the Bystander.* New York: HarperResource, 2003.

Fitzell, Susan Gringras. *Free The Children! Conflict Education For Strong and Peaceful Minds.* Connecticut: New Society Publishers, 1997.

Freedman, Judy S. *Easing the Teasing: Helping Your Child Cope with Name-Calling, Ridicule, and Verbal Bullying.* New York: McGraw-Hill / Contemporary Books, 2002.

Giannetti, Charlene C. and Margaret Sagarese. *Cliques: 8 Steps to Help Your Child Survive the Social Jungle.* New York: Broadway Books, 2001.

McCoy, Elin. *What To Do . . . When Kids Are Mean To Your Child.* New York: Reader's Digest Adult, 1997.

Olweus, Dan. *Bullying At School: What We Know and What We Can Do.* Massachusetts: Blackwell Publishers, 1994.

Simmons, Rachael. *Odd Girl Out: The Hidden Culture of Aggression in Girls.* New York: Harcourt, 2002.

Thompson, Michael, Lawrence J. Cohen, and Catherine O'Neill Grace. *Best Friends, Worst Enemies: Understanding the Social Lives of Children.* New York: Ballantine Books, 2001.

Thompson, Michael, Lawrence J. Cohen, and Catherine O'Neill Grace. *Mom, They're Teasing Me: Helping Your Child Solve Social Problems*. New York: Ballantine Books, 2002.

Wiseman, Rosalind. *Queen Bees and Wannabees: Helping Your Daughter Survive Cliques, Gossip, Boyfriends and Other Realities of Adolescence*. New York: Crown Publishers, 2002.

For Children:

Ages 4–8

Brown, Laurie Krasny and Marc Brown. *How To Be A Friend: A Guide to Making Friends and Keeping Them*. Massachusetts: Little Brown & Co., 2001.

Burnett, Karen Gedig. *Simon's Hook; A Story About Teases and Putdowns*. California: GR Publishing, 2002.

Cosby, Bill. *The Meanest Thing To Say*. New York: Scholastic Inc., 1997.

Lovell, Patty. *Stand Tall, Molly Lou Melon*. New York: Scholastic, 2002.

Thomas, Pat. *Stop Picking on Me: A First Look at Bullying*. New York: Barron's Educational Series, 2000.

Ages 8–12

Cohen-Posey, Kate. *How to Handle Bullies, Teasers and Other Meanies: A Book That Takes the Nuisance Out of Name Calling and Other Nonsense*. Florida: Rainbow Books, 1995.

Kaufman, Gershen, Raphael, Lev, and Espeland, Pamela. *Stick Up For Yourself! Every Kid's Guide to Personal Power and Positive Self-Esteem*. Minnesota: Free Spirit Publishing, 1999.

New Moon Books Girls Editorial Board. *Friendship: How to Make, Keep, and Grow Your Friendships*. New York: Crown Publishers, 1999.

Romain, Trevor. *Bullies Are a Pain in the Brain*. Minnesota: Free Spirit Publishing, 1997.

Romain, Trevor. *Cliques, Phonies, & Other Baloney*. Minnesota: Free Spirit Publishing, 1998.

Spinelli, Jerry. *Stargirl*. New York: Alfred A. Knopf, 2000.